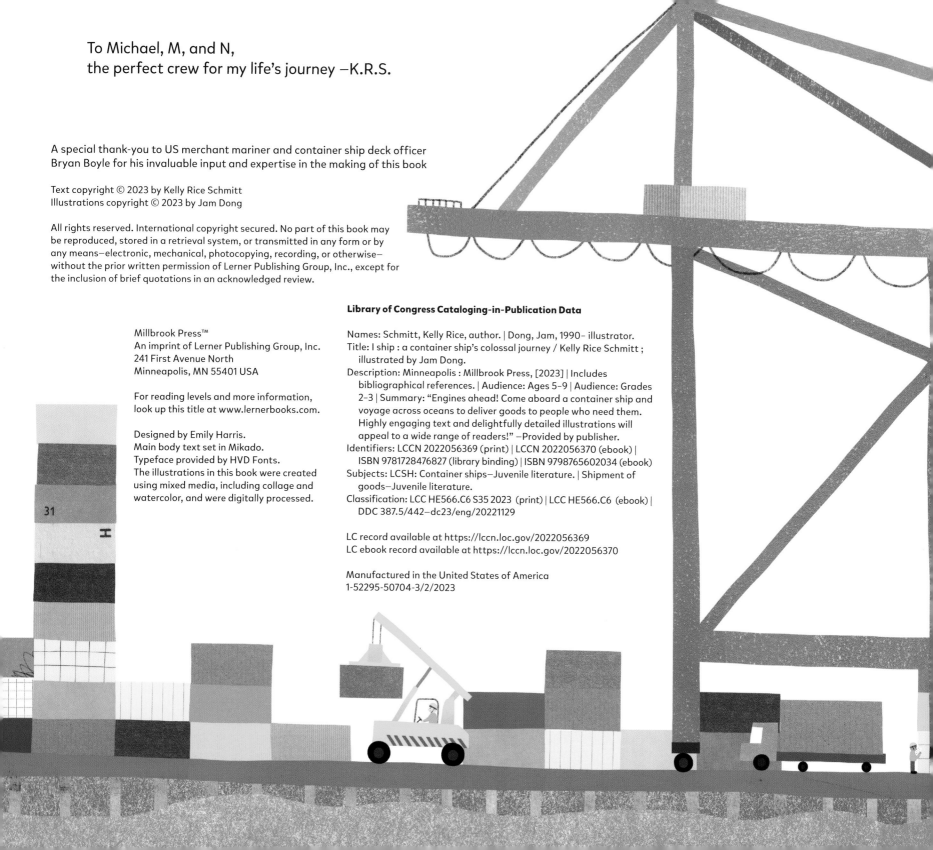

To Michael, M, and N,
the perfect crew for my life's journey —K.R.S.

A special thank-you to US merchant mariner and container ship deck officer
Bryan Boyle for his invaluable input and expertise in the making of this book

Millbrook Press™
An imprint of Lerner Publishing Group, Inc.
241 First Avenue North
Minneapolis, MN 55401 USA

For reading levels and more information,
look up this title at www.lernerbooks.com.

Designed by Emily Harris.
Main body text set in Mikado.
Typeface provided by HVD Fonts.
The illustrations in this book were created
using mixed media, including collage and
watercolor, and were digitally processed.

Library of Congress Cataloging-in-Publication Data

Names: Schmitt, Kelly Rice, author. | Dong, Jam, 1990– illustrator.
Title: I ship : a container ship's colossal journey / Kelly Rice Schmitt ;
    illustrated by Jam Dong.
Description: Minneapolis : Millbrook Press, [2023] | Includes
    bibliographical references. | Audience: Ages 5–9 | Audience: Grades
    2–3 | Summary: "Engines ahead! Come aboard a container ship and
    voyage across oceans to deliver goods to people who need them.
    Highly engaging text and delightfully detailed illustrations will
    appeal to a wide range of readers!" —Provided by publisher.
Identifiers: LCCN 2022056369 (print) | LCCN 2022056370 (ebook) |
    ISBN 9781728476827 (library binding) | ISBN 9798765602034 (ebook)
Subjects: LCSH: Container ships—Juvenile literature. | Shipment of
    goods—Juvenile literature.
Classification: LCC HE566.C6 S35 2023 (print) | LCC HE566.C6 (ebook) |
    DDC 387.5/442—dc23/eng/20221129

LC record available at https://lccn.loc.gov/2022056369
LC ebook record available at https://lccn.loc.gov/2022056370

Manufactured in the United States of America
1-52295-50704-3/2/2023

I SHIP

A Container Ship's Colossal Journey

written by Kelly Rice Schmitt

illustrated by Jam Dong

Millbrook Press / Minneapolis

CAROLINA

Made of steel,
colossal,
strong,
I ship around the world.

As I navigate through the straits,
past bay and bobbing buoy,
distant factories hum and hiss
preparing products for people.

My cargo is checked, packed, and stacked,
then rolled to the shipyard to meet me.

PARKER DOODLE

BOYLE

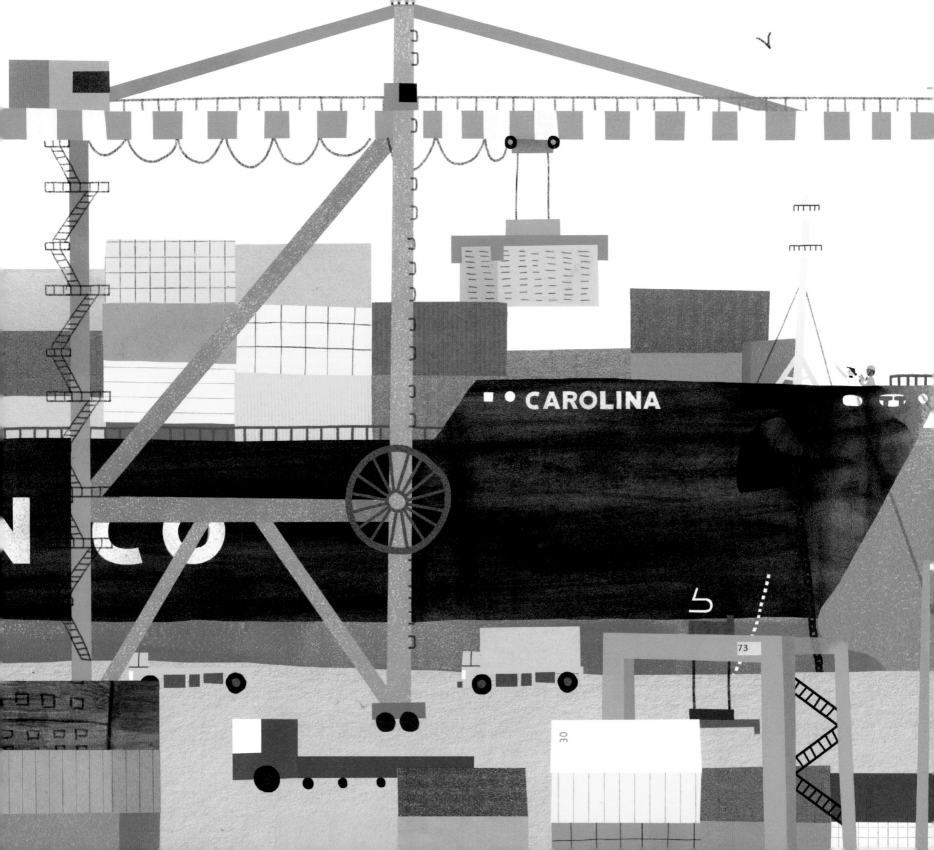

In port, my work begins.
Busy cranes lift from truck and train,
mariners yank, containers clang.

My captain checks, inspects.
"Safe and steady—she's seaworthy."
Crew is ready, weather's fine.
Tugboats chug, departure time!

Engines ahead!
HONK!

Sun on my deck,
birds at my stern,
I slice through salty seas.

KMN

I carry goods wherever I go,
helping the global economy flow.
Medicine, books, toys, and food—
I'm a floating treasure trove.
A sturdy container ship.

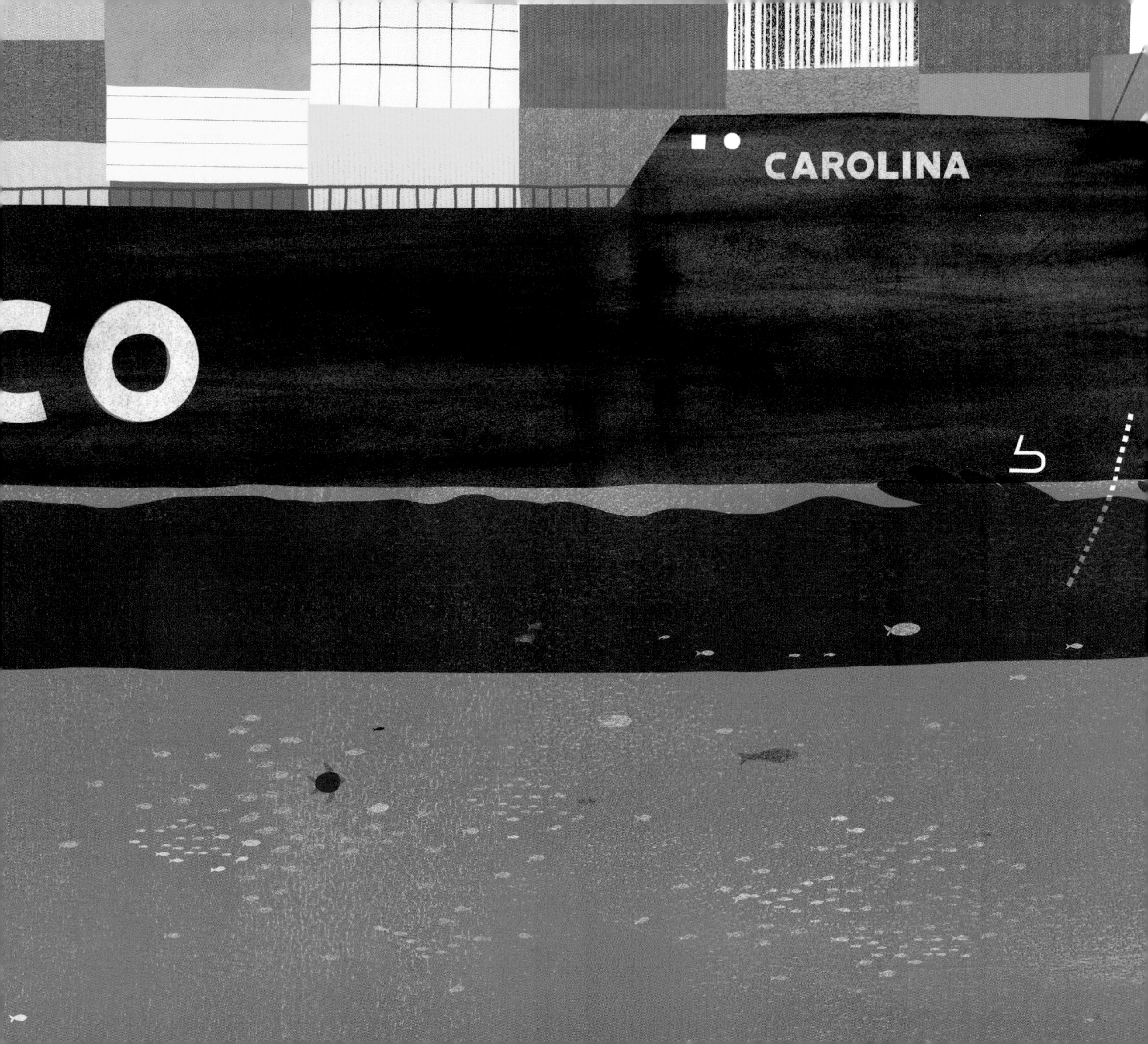
CAROLINA
CO

In some ways, I am massive,
a titan of the sea.

But alone in the ocean,
I'm tiny—
a drop of color
on a canvas of blue.

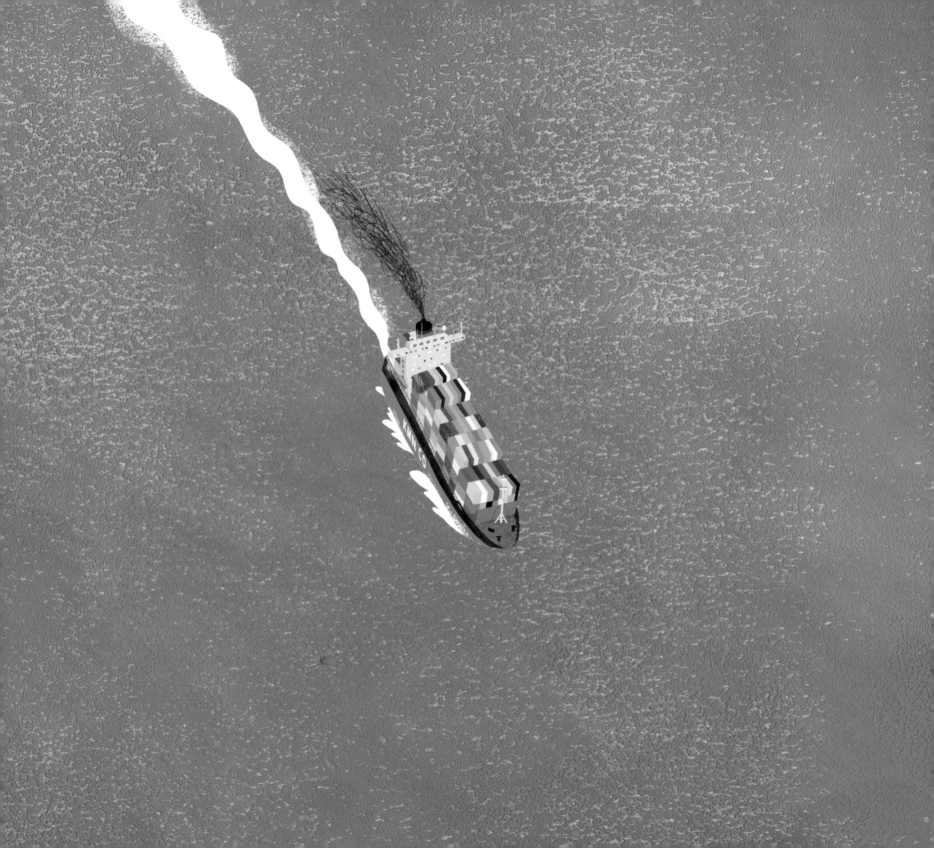

NICHOLAS

NASCO

Sea life might seem lonely,
but ships come together at canals.
"Ahoy!"

LNG BOP

CAROLINA

KMN CO

EJJ GETA

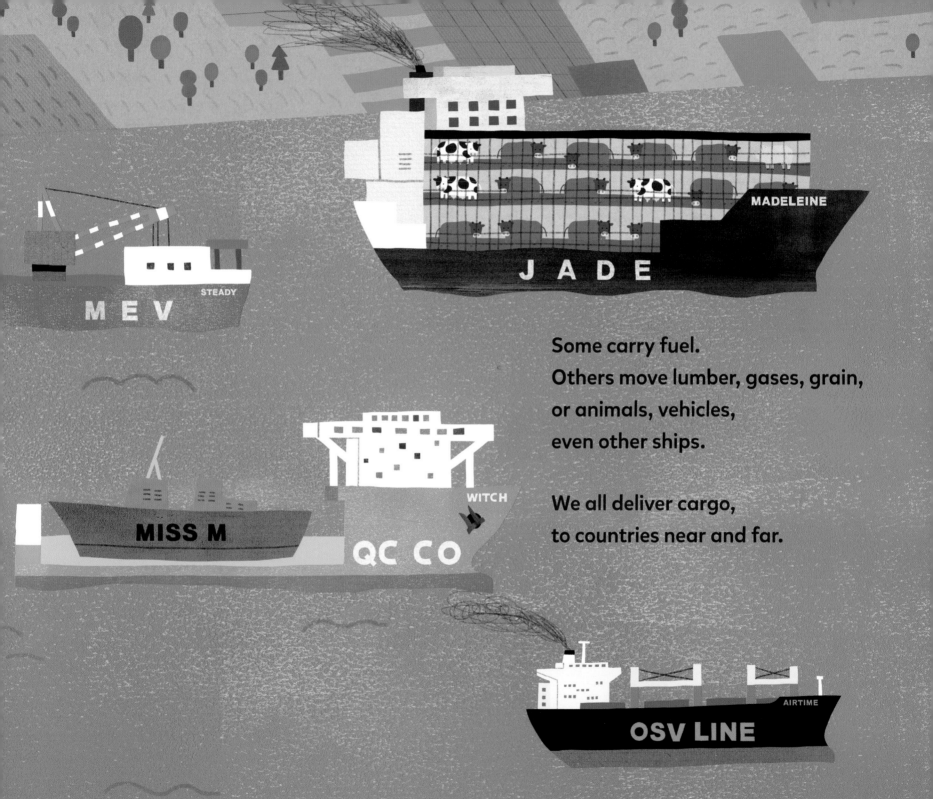

Some carry fuel.
Others move lumber, gases, grain,
or animals, vehicles,
even other ships.

We all deliver cargo,
to countries near and far.

This time, as I scoot in line,
something isn't right.

Vessels amassing,
no one passing . . .

a ship is stuck!
It's blocked the whole canal.

As time ticks, mariners twitch.
My captain paces the bridge.

The boss calls; we're on alert.
"Out of time," he says.
Reset course. Divert.

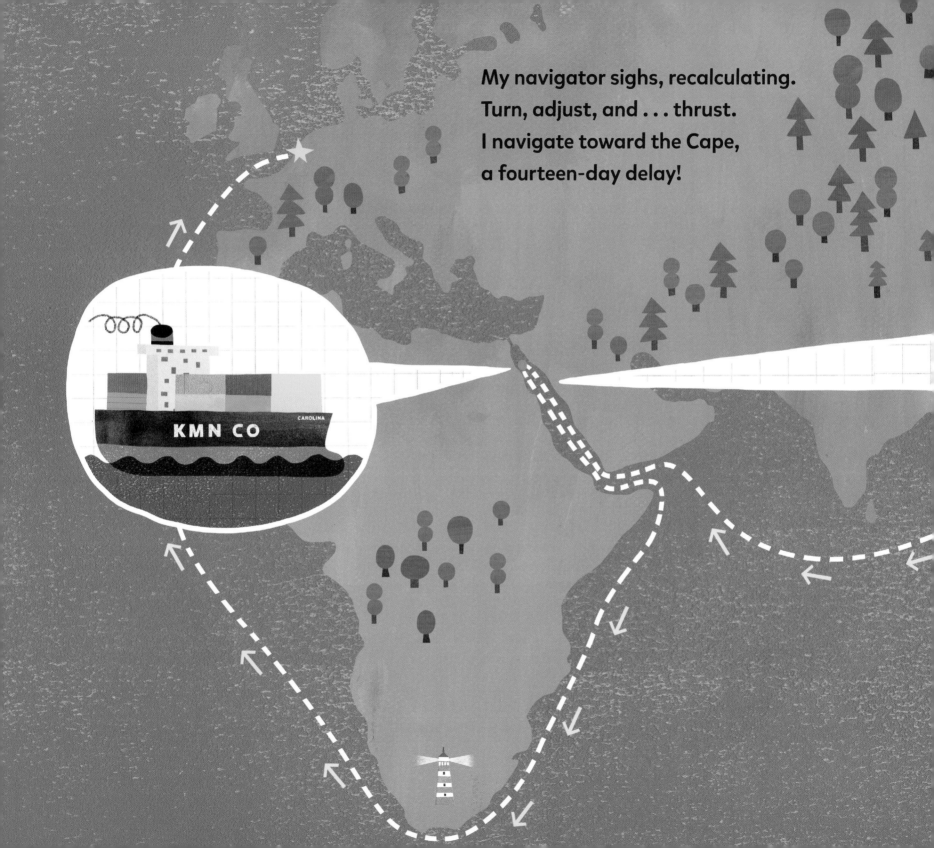

My navigator sighs, recalculating.
Turn, adjust, and . . . thrust.
I navigate toward the Cape,
a fourteen-day delay!

There's lifesaving medicine on board,
books for the first day of school.
Goods to keep the world going.
We must carry on.

Extra days, restless nights.
My crew is feeling blue.
But the ocean soothes like a lullaby.
Sway, spray, swoosh.
Sailing is smooth.

Until . . .

Thunder rumbles.

Crack!

Waves whip.

Smack!

"All hands inside!" my captain cries.
The helmsman takes the wheel.

We surrender to the storm.
Bow to the waves, we wait.

Endless pounding, pitch and roll.
My hull moans, groans with each bend.
The crew braces, eager for an end.

When the sea calms,
my crew is ready.
They scurry, counting, checking.
No damage! All is well.

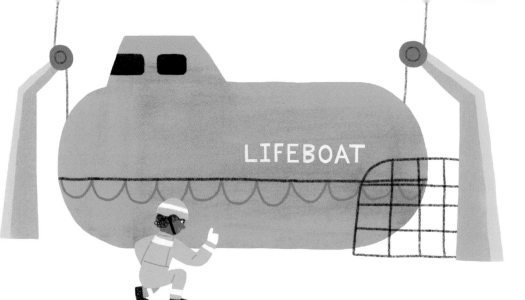

But we still must stop to bunker.
Fuel flows, worry grows.
Too many delays.
How will we make it on time?

I rev, churn,
chilly brine on my bow.

Winds providing,
currents guiding,
the sea is finally on our side!

Soon I'm gleaming, gliding
making up lost time.

The world is waiting.
Hospitals, schools,
factories, families—
everyone's counting on us.
It's our duty to deliver.
Almost there . . .

Cranes crank, unloading.
Clack, stack, and off they roll,
goods to feed, help, and heal.

Heads held high, my crew heaves a sigh.
Delivery complete!

KELLY

Trade is flowing, the world keeps going.
But oceans away, new ports await.
So once again, I load up and carry on
because . . .

RABBIT   M B K C O

CAROLINA

I ship!

Why Do Countries Trade?

Because the countries of the world have different temperatures and land types (such as forests, rivers, mountains, and deserts), they have different resources and different needs. Resources are items a country can grow, collect, or make with its land and skills. Some natural resources include fruit and vegetables, wood, fish, gold, oil, coffee, or sheep. Human-made resources include computers, cars, clothing, and medicine. Countries trade so that each nation can sell extra resources and buy the things it doesn't have. For example, a country with few waterways may need to buy fish from a country with more oceans, lakes, or rivers. An important part of trading is cost. Making or growing an item may be much less expensive in one part of the world. Another country might choose to buy and ship that item where it's needed rather than making or growing that item itself. Because of international trade, we can have fresh fruits and vegetables all year, shipped from areas where they're in season. We can also buy special foods, toys, and clothes that are only made in other countries. We live in a true global economy—shipping connects every place in the world!

Challenges of Intermodal Container Shipping

One drawback of container shipping is its environmental impact. Container ships travel long distances, creating more air, water, and noise pollution than the travel involved if goods are bought locally. Sometimes containers fall off ships and sink to the ocean floor. If a sunken container breaks open, its contents pollute the ocean and coastlines where the items wash ashore. Environmental problems can also happen if water emptied from a ship's ballast tanks, which hold seawater to help balance the ship, accidentally transports bacteria, sea creatures, or plants to places they don't belong.

Another challenge of international shipping is our dependence on the supply chain, the network of businesses goods pass through from producer to end user. Just a single delay can cause ripple effects throughout the world. For example, in 2021 the *Ever Given*, a container ship traveling from Malaysia to the Netherlands, became stuck in the Suez Canal, an Egyptian waterway connecting the Red Sea and the Mediterranean Sea. With as many as seventy ships crossing per day, the cargo moved through the Suez makes up about 12 percent of global trade or an estimated $9 billion! This blockage caused global delays when ships stuck in the canal were late arriving to their destinations, making not only their deliveries late but also the goods waiting to be loaded at the ships' next loading ports. Other goods made with parts from many countries—such as cars and computers—were delayed too.

Benefits of Intermodal Container Shipping

I Ship focuses on trade happening via intermodal containers, which are 20- or 40-foot (6 or 12 m) steel boxes that connect to ships, trains, and trucks. They can easily be transferred from one vehicle to another as they go from factory to final customer across water or land. Invented in the 1950s, the modern intermodal container revolutionized the way goods move around the world. These containers make loading and unloading standardized, no matter what kind of cargo is inside them. And that makes shipping faster and easier. Before containerization, loading and unloading items took longer than crossing the oceans—it could take up to three weeks to load or unload a ship! Strong workers had to use pulleys or physically carry heavy goods on and off ships. Today, modern ports use enormous, specialized cranes that zip back and forth. These cranes move containers from truck or train to yard to ship with ease. (Some ships are even self-loading with cranes built into their decks!) Now even the largest vessels can be loaded or unloaded in about one day. Intermodal containers also save money. Because they are a uniform size, more goods can fit into the same cargo-holding space. And that means more goods can fit on one ship, so the cost of shipping each individual item on the ship is lower.

Glossary of Shipping and Trading Terms

ahoy: a call used to attract attention from another ship, often used like "hello"

ballast tanks: tanks in a ship that can be pumped full of seawater to help improve the ship's stability or to change how deep the ship sits in the water

bay: a body of water partially surrounded by land but having a wide opening to the sea

bow: the front part of a ship

brine: salt water

bunker: to fill a ship's fuel tanks

buoy: a floating object anchored to the seafloor that is used to warn ships of underwater hazards such as shallow waters or coral reefs

canal: a human-made waterway for ships

captain: the leader and commanding officer of a ship

cargo: goods carried on a ship

container: a metal box that holds goods on an intermodal container ship

course: the direction or path of travel for a ship

crew: everyone working on a ship

current: the flow of water in a certain direction

deck: a platform running across the top of the ship, forming a floor

divert: to change direction and take a new path

engines ahead: a command to move the ship forward

global economy: activities related to the making and selling of goods and services between countries

goods: physical objects that people need or want

hands: members of a ship's crew

helmsman: crew member who steers the ship

hull: the frame or body of a ship

land ho: an old marine term meaning land has been sighted

mariner: a sailor; a person who helps run a ship

navigator: a person who decides which direction a ship needs to go to get to a destination

on board: on the ship

pitch and roll: when a ship rocks up and down (pitch) and swings from side to side (roll)

port: a place where ships load and unload cargo

portside: the left side of a ship when facing toward the front of the ship

seaworthy: safe and ready for a sea voyage

shipyard: a place where ships are built and repaired; also known as a yard

starboard: the right side of a ship when facing toward the front of the ship

stern: the rear end of a ship

strait: a relatively narrow passageway connecting two large bodies of water

trade: the business of buying and selling goods

tugboat: a powerful boat used for towing and pushing ships

vessel: a watercraft bigger than a rowboat; ships or boats

Join the Crew! Shipping and Trading Jobs

Are you fascinated by shipping or how goods move around the world? Here are some careers to consider if you want to work at sea or in international trade:

Jobs at Sea

captain: the lead deck officer and commander of the whole ship. The captain sets course to achieve a safe and on time voyage, maintains logs of the journey and cargo, and ensures the overall safety of the crew and cargo.

deck department: crew members responsible for the navigation and maintenance of the ship and its cargo. They stand watch, navigate the ship, conduct security rounds, oversee load and unload, and communicate with the port and other vessels. Team members include the deck officers, bosun, and able bodied seamen (ABs).

engine department: responsible for operating, maintaining, and repairing the ship's engines, machinery, and other major systems such as electricity, lights, fuel, refrigeration, water, and air conditioning. Team members include the chief engineer, engine officers, qualified member of the engine department (QMED), electrician, wiper, and deck engine utility (DEU).

steward department: crew members who cook and serve food for the crew and handle housekeeping for the ship

Jobs on Land

cargo planner: a businessperson who calculates where to place the containers in the ship and in what order to ensure safety and fast loading and unloading

exporter or importer: someone who sells goods from their country to other countries (exporter) or buys goods from other countries to sell in theirs (importer)

longshoreman: a dock worker who oversees the loading and unloading of containers onto or off the vessels and any other intermodal vehicles in the terminal. They ensure containers are undamaged and secure to keep the crew and cargo safe on their journey. They work outside year-round, regardless of weather, and may operate heavy machinery such as cranes.

marine engineer or naval architect: both of these jobs are performed by engineering specialists who design, build, and repair ships. They use computers and other tools to help them design vessels. Sometimes they go to sea to conduct tests or maintain existing ships.

maritime pilot: a ship operator based at a port or canal with expert knowledge of local waterways. The pilot boards ships to help the crew safely maneuver narrow or shallow channels and rivers during arrival and departure at ports and canals.

ship operator: works with a ship's crew to ensure they are on time and following the law. They report updates to customers with containers on the ship, oversee the ship's schedule, calculate when and where to refuel, handle important paperwork, and more.

train engineer: a train operator moving intermodal containers on railways

truck driver: an operator of trucks moving intermodal containers across land

Fast Facts about Intermodal Container Shipping

- An estimated 80 to 90 percent of the world's global trade moves via ship.

- As of 2022, the United States imported about 15 percent of the total annual food supply, including 32 percent of fresh vegetables, 55 percent of fresh fruit, and 94 percent of fresh seafood from more than 200 countries.

- Each container has a unique identification number to help the importing and exporting companies track their goods. Once loaded, containers are sealed and locked to ensure the safety of the contents.

- As of 2022, there were more than 5,500 modern container ships in circulation. They can hold anywhere from 1,000 to nearly 24,000 20-foot (6 m) containers.

- Container ship sizes are measured in TEUs, or twenty-foot equivalent units.

- A semitruck you see on the highway usually holds one 40-foot (12 m) container, which is equal to 2 TEUs. That means it would take 12,000 semitrucks to hold the same volume as a ship holding 24,000 TEUs!

- The largest container ships are more than 1,312 feet (400 m) long. That's taller than the height of the Eiffel Tower in Paris, France, and almost as tall as the Empire State Building in New York City.

- Container ships are so large they can be seen from the International Space Station!

See It for Yourself! Recommended Videos

"Bryan Boyle"
The YouTube channel of US merchant mariner Bryan Boyle
https://www.youtube.com/c/BryanBoyle

"Chain Reaction: Why Global Supply Chains May Never Be the Same"
A 2022 Wall Street Journal documentary by Christopher Mims
https://www.youtube.com/watch?v=1KtTAb9Tl6E

"Unique Look Inside One of the Biggest Container Ships in the World"
A 2020 excerpt from Richard Hammond's Big! on Discovery Australia
https://www.youtube.com/watch?v=pNdughfkDbM

How Do Container Ships Float?

How can something so big and heavy float? It's all about *buoyancy*—an object's ability to float in liquid. Buoyancy is determined by two key factors.

1. Displacement: the amount of water an object pushes aside

2. Density: how tightly packed together the stuff that makes up an object is

An object floats when the water the object pushes aside, or displaces, is greater than the weight of the object. Shipbuilders design ships to displace a lot of water to account for their huge size and weight. The secret is in the shape of the ship and the amount of air inside it. Ships have long, wide bottoms and deep sides (known as the *hull*) to maximize their surface area—the amount of space the outside of an object touches. More surface area means more water will be displaced because more parts of the ship touch the water, pushing it aside. Although container ships are made of steel, they are mostly hollow and filled with air, which helps keep their density and weight low compared to the amount of water they displace with their large surface area.

Want to see buoyancy in action? Download the activity guide at www.lernerbooks.com/iship for experiments!

For a complete bibliography and more, visit http://www.kellyriceschmitt.com.

Seek and Find

Grab your binoculars, mate! It's your turn to check and inspect . . . this book. Can you find all the objects shown here?